I AM GOLDEN

By New York Times–bestselling author
EVA CHEN

Illustrated by
SOPHIE DIAO

FEIWEL AND FRIENDS · NEW YORK

A FEIWEL AND FRIENDS BOOK
An imprint of Macmillan Publishing Group, LLC
120 Broadway, New York, NY 10271 • mackids.com

Library of Congress Cataloging-in-Publication Data is available

First edition, 2022
Book design by Aram Kim
The illustrations for this book were created digitally
Photos courtesy of Eva Chen and Sophie Diao
Feiwel and Friends logo designed by Filomena Tuosto
Printed and bound in Mexico by Procesos y Acabados en Artes Gráficas S.A. de C.V.

ISBN 978-1-250-84205-3
3 5 7 9 10 8 6 4

This book is for all the golden children out there.

You are dreamers, doers, and makers.
Your difference is your superpower.

And—as always—to my parents,
who gave me the world.
—E.C.

For my mama, baba, and brother—you are golden.
—S.D.

We named you Mei.

 Not *May* like the month. *Měi*, which means **beautiful**.

Like the country we live in now—*Měi Guó*, America.

What do you see when you look in the mirror, Mei? Do you see beauty?

We see eyes that point toward the sun, that give us the warmth and joy of a thousand rays when you smile. We see hair as inky black and smooth as a peaceful night sky. We see skin brushed with gold.

We see the hopes and dreams
of your ancestors when we look at you.

We journeyed into the unknown to give you a new path to trailblaze. In this upside-down world, clever child, you have become our teacher and translator.

Our words won't always be enough to comfort you. And we won't be able to be with you every step of the way.

We know you feel alone sometimes.

People tell you that you're different and you can't be one of them.

But we promise . . . there is power in being different.

Are you ready, brave Mei, to hear about your secret power?

You are never alone.

You carry a golden flame inside you, and it's always with you.

You are made of dragons, of phoenixes, of jade rabbits, and of monkey kings.

You are the lotus flower unfurling—triumphant and bright—in the darkest water. You are the first bamboo stalk, piercing the soil, that will overtake the sky.

Your voice is the call of the magpie, joyful and unapologetic.

It's a strange world we live in—people will call you different with one breath and then say that we all look the same with the next angry breath.

But they don't know that each of our golden flames flickers distinctly. That our stories are infinitely unique.

We are artists, scientists, athletes.

We are dancers, teachers, inventors.

We are architects, actors, writers.

You can hear all our stories when we gather as a family.

There will be celebrations—oh, we love to celebrate!—with plate upon plate of delectable deliciousness that will tickle all your senses.

The hot pop and sizzle of garlic in a wok.

The lazy curls of steam from freshly kneaded bao.

The sesame balls that will leave your fingers slick and sweet.

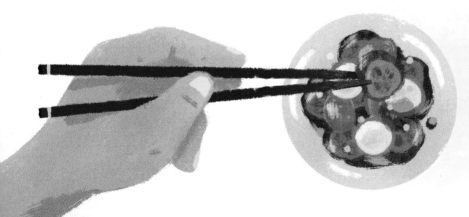

We gather to hope, to dream, and to sing your praises, Mei. To send love to your popo and gong-gong, who are not in Měi Guó with us. To pay tribute to those we've loved and lost along the way as oceans and worlds and cultures separated us.

Have we taught you the word *mìng* yet?

It means destiny, Mei. Our destiny was **you**.

Our mìng is to be the keepers of your flame,

to guide you as best we can.

We see you. We see your golden heart.

You are beauty, but so much more.

You are strength. You are power. You, Mei, are golden.

Say it with us. Believe it.

"I AM GOLDEN."

A Note from the Author

Growing up, I felt like I lived in two different worlds. There was "School Eva"—I'd chatter in English to my classmates, rejoice when it was pizza day for lunch, and obsess over whatever boy band was trending at the time. But come 3 P.M., when I would get picked up, I would be re-immersed in a world that centered around being Chinese. I'd speak Mandarin to my parents, I'd warble along with whatever Chinese songs my parents listened to, and we'd spend weekends grocery shopping on Mott Street in New York City's Chinatown or eating soup dumplings in a hole-in-the-wall restaurant in Flushing, Queens.

I never questioned that this bifurcated existence was anything other than normal until a classmate bullied me in grade school. I was about eight years old and the fellow student pulled the corners of his eyes and made some comments in a singsong voice during recess. The boy was popular—and I most definitely wasn't—so all the other kids laughed along with him. Today, I still live close by the school. When I pass the playground where it happened, decades later, the memory washes over me as though it were yesterday.

Today, as a mother to three half-Chinese children, I hope that they will never experience that sting of otherness, the swirl of confusion, of questioning whether they belong. But I'm also deeply aware that it is—unfortunately, despite all I can do to protect them from it—an eventuality.

I wrote *I Am Golden* during the COVID-19 pandemic, during a meteoric rise in anti-Asian sentiment. I feared for my parents' safety, telling them to wear sunglasses (and hats . . . and scarves) so that people wouldn't see that they were Asian. And yet, during this time, I gained a deeper understanding of my parents as well. One night, I asked my mother what the hardest part of coming to America was. Her response? The loneliness. Of being in between worlds. That sacrifice she and my father made—which countless other immigrants have made—for their children was the seed of an idea for this book. I wrote the book to celebrate their story—as a love letter to my parents, to their dedication, strength, and commitment to their family. And I wrote the book as a wish for my children, so that they may understand their magic and power.

And that, reader, is my wish for your children too. May they understand their strength, may they understand their family history in all its unique beauty, and may they know that they are truly golden.

A Note from the Illustrator

My parents left China in the late eighties, moving first to Stuttgart, Germany for a few years before immigrating to Missouri, where I was born. I've always admired their courage in starting over in not one, but *two* new countries, adapting to a new culture and language each time. Even once they got to the United States and started a family, we moved to a new state every couple of years as my father sought a better life for us through his career.

I loved learning, but I hated always being the new kid at school—especially when I was the only Asian student in the class. My newness was exacerbated by the differences pointed out by my classmates and teachers, and it wasn't until I got much older that I learned to cherish my Chinese heritage for its richness and for connecting me to my family—especially all of my other relatives, who still live in China.

This book has been an incredible opportunity to illustrate my experience, which is so very similar to Mei's, and share it with all the children who are still learning to embrace the things that make them unique and brilliant.